Me with You

For Demps, always me with you   —KD

For two Grandpas and a Pop-Pop   —CD

Me with You

Kristy Dempsey • Christopher Denise

SCHOLASTIC INC.
New York Toronto London Auckland
Sydney Mexico City New Delhi Hong Kong

We're a pair beyond compare,
a rare and special two,
in all the ways that I am me
and you're completely you.

When I am me, I'm dressed for tea
with you beside my chair.
Your head held high, you nibble pie
with fancy silverware.

When I am me, I'm swinging
over puddles from a rope,
and you stand ready with a sponge
and bucket full of soap.

I'm me when I am chasing down
the wind that swiped your hat

or cheering for another run
when you are up to bat.

I'm me when I am sick in bed,
all feverish with flu,
so you stay close to care for me
and watch the whole night through.

When you are tickling ivories,
it's me who sings off-key.

When you are wrapping presents,
I hang trimmings on the tree.

When you are in the garden,
I'm prepared to tip the spout.
Together we know how to grow
a rainbow from a sprout.

I'm me when I am off at camp,
but you have stayed at home

to be the kind of you
that you can be when you're alone.

I'm me on an adventure,
digging treasure from the sand,
and when the path is rocky,
you are there to hold my hand.

Whenever I am not so nice,
and selfish with my stuff,
you're the one who loves me
and forgives me if I'm gruff.

If I decide to run away,
then you come running too,
to talk me into going back
before the day is through.

On days when being me feels like
the sky was painted black,
you and I together roll
along a brighter track.

And though I'll find new ways
of being me my whole life through,
my favorite me will always be . . .

when I am me with you.

PATRICIA LEE GAUCH, EDITOR

ISBN 978-0-545-34046-5

12 11 10 9 8 7 6 5 4 3 2 1   11 12 13 14 15 16/0

Printed in the U.S.A.   08

This edition first printing, January 2011

Design by Semadar Megged
Text set in Goudy Old Style
The art for this book was created using Photoshop CS3 with a Wacom Intuos 2 tablet.